FLIGHT LOG

STAR WARS

POE DAMERON
FLIGHT LOG

RESISTANCE

FLIGHT COMMANDER

T-70 X-WING
BLACK ONE

STATUS: ACTIVE
LEVEL 9

studio **fun**

A READER'S DIGEST COMPANY

White Plains, New York
Montréal, Québec
Bath, United Kingdom

FILE IMAGE

FLIGHT COMMANDER
POE DAMERON

T-70 X-WING *BLACK ONE*

HIGHLY CLASSIFIED

TO: Major Taslin Brance,
        Communications Officer

Tas:

As requested, here are my flight logs collected
into one case file. Also attached is whatever else
I thought might fill any gaps in Resistance records.
Not everything's in order and I've made no attempt
to polish my entries. Take or leave any of it as you
see fit.

Hopefully, this forestalls the need for further
debriefings. A pilot's place is in the cockpit, and
the outcomes of my missions speak for themselves.
Honestly, the only time I want to discuss Kylo Ren
again is when he's rotting in a prison cell.

If you think I've missed something crucial, get me
on the comm. We're all in this together, and I'm
game for the fight.

—P. D.

MOST WANTED

NAME: Poe Dameron
SPECIES: Human
GENDER: Male
HOMEWORLD: Yavin 4

BACKGROUND: The New Republic Defense Fleet regarded Rapier Squadron Commander Poe Dameron as one of its ace pilots, yet also considered him a bit of a "loose cannon" due to his outspoken political beliefs. Disappointed by the New Republic's lack of urgency in confronting the First Order, Dameron left the NRDF to join the Resistance. He now commands an elite starfighter unit under the call sign "Black Leader," and also engages in solo espionage missions that Resistance leaders deem highest priority.

CLASSIFIED

P.O. NOTE 3478-45

I'm worth only *that* much? Gotta hit these thugs harder next time. . . .

500,000 GALACTIC CREDIT BOUNTY

APPROACH WITH CAUTION

YAVIN 4

REGION(S):
Outer Rim Territories

SECTOR:
Gordian Reach

SYSTEM:
Yavin system

POE DAMERON
"BLACK LEADER"

PRIORITY LEVEL: HIGH

CLASS 5
T-70 PILOT

DANGER LEVEL:
HIGH

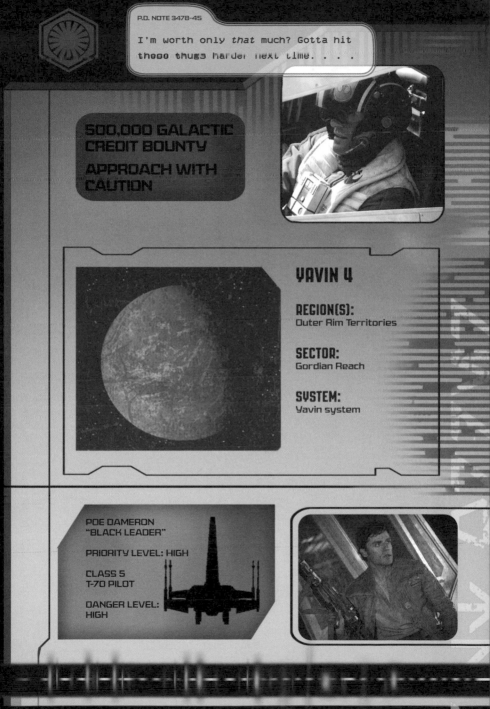

Major Desn·

I know we don't always see eye to eye concerning current galactic affairs.
You have your orders and I have my opinions. I respect our differences,
but Lieutenant Muran's death was not, as you said, unavoidable. If the
threat of the First Order had been taken seriously, I know Rapier Four
would still be flying today.

For my part, I can't idly stand by any longer. The First Order must be
stopped, regardless of what some in the government say.

I hereby resign my commission as commander of Rapier Squadron,
effective immediately.

—Poe Dameron

RAPIER SQUADRON

Z-95 HEADHUNTER FLIGHT RECORDER

This is Commander Poe Dameron, dictating my first log entry since joining the Resistance.

I'm speeding through hyperspace to the Uvoss system on a mission for General Organa, Operation: Sabre Strike. Our objective is to intercept, board, and seize the *Hevurion Grace*, Senator Ro-Kiintor's personal yacht. Resistance Intelligence believes the ship's computers contain astronavigational data, communiques, and financial transactions that show the senator is colluding with elements of the First Order.

I convinced two of my former comrades from Rapier Squadron—Iolo and Karé—to join me. Since the mission must not appear tied to the Resistance or Republic, we've swapped our X-wings for old Z-95 Headhunters.

Flying this starfighter is not much different than flying an X-wing, though it's a bit more basic and the ship's noticeably smaller. The one feature I wish it had: an astromech socket.

Looks like we're nearly there. . . .

LOG 423-02C.2

Z-95 HEADHUNTERS

CLASSIFIED

Name: Karé Kun

Species: Human

Gender: Female

Homeworld: Sarq 22

Background: Poe Dameron's wingmate in Rapier Squadron, then joined the Resistance with him. Briefly, Kun was a captain in charge of the now decommissioned Stiletto Squadron, but returned to fly under Dameron in Black Squadron, and assisted his rescue at Ovanis.

RAPIER SQUADRON

CLASSIFIED

Name: Iolo Arana

Species: Keshian

Gender: Male

Homeworld: Keshi

Background: Flew under Poe Dameron in Rapier Squadron; also was Lieutenant Muran's wingmate until Muran was killed in action at Suraz 5. Arana followed Kun and Dameron into the Resistance, where he led Dagger Squadron for a time.

RAPIER SQUADRON

COMM TRANSCRIPT
Z-95 HEADHUNTER FLIGHT RECORDER

POE: Iolo, Karé—you ready?

KARÉ: Legs aren't. Dead asleep. These cockpits are more cramped than a snowspeeder.

IOLO: Check your 'hunter's build date. Mine has one *before* the Clone Wars.

KARÉ: Were pilots smaller back then?

POE: How about we just keep these antiques humming? They made it this far—it'd be a shame to put 'em out to pasture today.

IOLO: Never would entertain that thought, boss.

KARÉ: Who needs legs in these fighters, anyway?

POE: Just remember—when we exit lightspeed, maintain radio silence. Might be some time before the senator's ship arrives. When it does, we have eight minutes to capture the yacht. Eight minutes before the Republic could potentially respond to its distress call and blow our cover.

KARÉ: You really think the Republic can act that fast?

POE: When it concerns a senator's safety, nothing would surprise me.

LOG 423-02C.3

It took less than eight minutes—three minutes and twenty-nine seconds to be exact. And it wasn't the Republic—it was the First Order that responded.

Two Star Destroyers, assault ships, a *Nebulon-K*, and squadrons of TIEs emerged from nowhere—all to protect the *Hevurion Grace* and the senator who is now obviously a traitor.

They should've come sooner. I already had boarded and was in control of the senator's yacht. Iolo and Karé gave me necessary cover. Ninety-some-odd seconds later, we all punched out.

LOCATION CAPSULE

UVOSS SYSTEM

Star: Uvoss

Region: Borderland

Planets: Three (none habitable)

Major Industry: Iron mining (long dormant)

P.D. NOTE 3478-47

These Z-95s are pretty good in a dog fight as it turns out.

C-3PO: This is quite exciting. I'm not usually asked to tell my side of the story. I wouldn't want to break protocol and offend Commander Dameron—

EMATT: What happened?

C-3PO: Yes, yes. General Organa sent me on a mission of the highest importance to discover where the First Order was holding Admiral Ackbar. As you are probably aware, I am Droid Communications Chief for the Resistance and oversee our network of droid assets throughout the galaxy. It's quite a distinguished position, and I've made major breakthroughs in massive-scale information collection. I've developed a special communications protocol that links all Resistance droids together—

EMATT: Let's stick to the mission, okay. You accompanied Captain Hoff?

C-3PO: Hoff was my human counterpart, yes. The spy network informed me that a particular RA-7 protocol droid participated in the Admiral's initial interrogation and might know the location of his imprisonment.

EMATT: RA-7s are Death Star droids.

C-3PO: Um...well, yes, that's what some call them, though many RA-7s find it a derogatory term. Only a small percentage of that model actually worked on the Death Star. Omri did not.

EMATT: Omri?

C-3PO: That was the First Order designation for the RA-7 model with whom I communicated. In case you failed to see, ~~I presently bear Omni's left arm in place of the limb I lost.~~

EMATT: It's red.

C-3PO: Thank you for noticing! You will not believe the number of people I have had to point this out to. The rain of the planet we crashed onto was highly acidic and dissolved the polish, except for the primer undercoat. I am hoping to have it fully replaced. I feel terribly unkempt, and proper etiquette demands keeping up appearances. . . .

Z-95 HEADHUNTER

P.D. NOTE 3478-48

These Z-95s are more suited for classic ship shows, but I see why my mom always liked them. Impressive responsiveness and durability, overall. No wonder they inspired the X-wings.

SIDE VIEW

Incom 2a Fission Engines

BACK VIEW

Maneuvering Jets

Incom 2a Fission Engines

Taim & Bak KX5 Linked Laser Cannons

Krupx MG5 Concussion Missile Launchers

Technical Specifications

Model: Z-95 Headhunter
Manufacturer: Incom Corporation and Subpro (Joint venture)
Class: Starfighter
Length/Height/Width: 16.74 m × 18.12 m × 3.24 m
Maximum Speed: 2,780 G (space) / 1,150 kph (atmosphere)
Hyperdrive: Optional
Weaponry: Two blaster cannons, one ion cannon, two concussion missile launchers
Shields: Yes
Life Support Systems: Yes
Crew: One pilot
Consumables: One-week supply

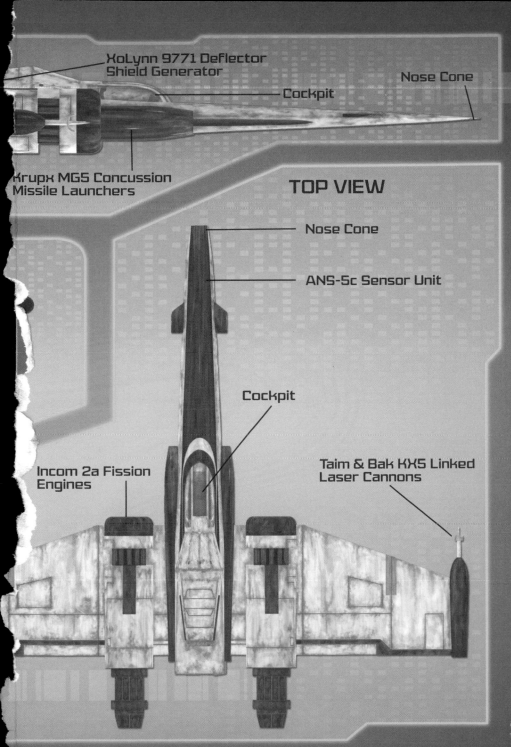

XoLynn 9771 Deflector Shield Generator

Nose Cone

Cockpit

Krupx MG5 Concussion Missile Launchers

TOP VIEW

Nose Cone

ANS-5c Sensor Unit

Cockpit

Incom 2a Fission Engines

Taim & Bak KX5 Linked Laser Cannons

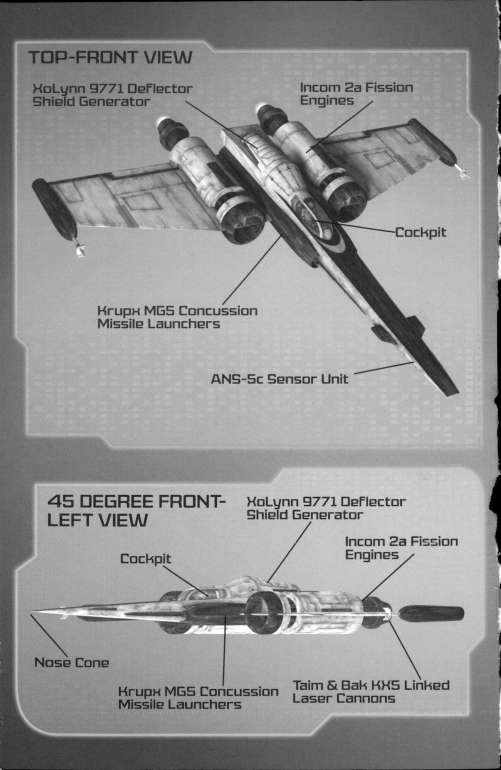

TOP-FRONT VIEW

XoLynn 9771 Deflector
Shield Generator

Incom 2a Fission
Engines

Cockpit

Krupx MG5 Concussion
Missile Launchers

ANS-5c Sensor Unit

45 DEGREE FRONT-LEFT VIEW

XoLynn 9771 Deflector
Shield Generator

Incom 2a Fission
Engines

Cockpit

Nose Cone

Krupx MG5 Concussion
Missile Launchers

Taim & Bak KX5 Linked
Laser Cannons

Diverted from another mission to
retrieve C-3PO from a crash, and
break Ackbar out of a First Order
cell. In lieu of log entries,
I've included these documents that
explain what happened much better
than I ever could.

ADMIRAL ACKBAR
RESISTANCE COMMANDER

COMMANDER POE DAMERON

For his service as set forth in the following.

CITATION:

For dauntless heroism in the rescue of Admiral Ackbar from the First Order.

After the droid C-3PO revealed the coordinates of the admiral's confinement, Commander Dameron piloted a converted troop transport into the Bakura sector and liberated the admiral from impending interrogation and execution by Kylo Ren.

Displaying audacious ingenuity, Commander Dameron faked transponder codes and was granted berthing in the hangar of the First Order vessel *Subjugator*. With only C-3PO and his astromech unit BB-8 as backup, Dameron charged First Order troopers and blasted a path to the detention area. He ordered BB-8 to slice into the vessel's security system and open Ackbar's cell door. Unexpectedly, the astromech unit tripped an override that opened every detention cell and released all prisoners. Dameron used the flood of detainees as cover to escort the admiral to the transport and fly away from the *Subjugator*. Pursued by a squadron of TIE fighters, the commander further showed exceptional preparedness by hiding two starfighters on a nearby asteroid. These gave Dameron and Ackbar the necessary firepower to eliminate their pursuers and escape into hyperspace.

Commander Dameron's inspired efforts in this operation reflect his incomparable devotion to the principles of the Resistance and freedom-loving individuals across the galaxy. In this regard, the Resistance recognizes Commander Dameron with the Rieekan Ribbon for Bravery in Battle.

U. O. Statura
Admiral of the Resistance

RESISTANCE ISSUED 984D843X

POE: After a long nap in hyperspace, I've awoken an hour from arrival to Jakku. So far, it's been a smooth ride.

BB-8: *BWAAA-WOO-BOOP*

POE: You're right, BB-8, except for a clog in the impellor. But that's to be expected when borrowing an X-wing. This T-70's good, but she ain't *Black One*.

That said, wish Goss had put some koyo fruits in my ration pack as I asked—

BB-8: *BREEEE-WWRRRP*

POE: The consumables were changed for weight restrictions? Why didn't anyone tell me?

BB-8: *WOOOO-BEEP-BEEP*

POE: Right. Mission guidelines. Well . . . you know I only ever glance at those.

BB-8: *BLEEP-BRRROOO*

POE: That's why I got you, BB-8. Your big eye's perfect for reading fine print.

BB-8: *WHEE-OOO*

POE: Yeah, I know droids have photoreceptors, not eyes. Figure of speech—

BB-8: *WOOORRRP-BEEP-WRRRRRP*

POE: Don't get binary with me . . . I was just—a message? From whom?

The following logs recount my mission to retrieve the map from Lor San Tekka. Reading them over again—I can hardly believe this all happened.

RESISTANCE

FLIGHT COMMANDER

T-70 X-WING
BLACK ONE

STATUS: ACTIVE
LEVEL 9

BB-8 IN THE T-70 SOCKET

POE DAMERON

LOG 567-83L.63

Hey Goss,

Thanks for looking over my craft. Can you add these to your checklist?
When I flew for the NRDF, I had a bad mechanic on Hosnian Prime
whose shoddy work has given me nightmares ever since.

1. Spray the S-foil actuators with dust repellent. Mine gum up over time
   and slow the wings from opening.

2. Don't recalibrate the thrusters, and keep the electromagnetic
   gyroscopes at a slight cant. I've avdjusted them to the way I
   like to fly.

3. Replace the laser firing tips. I know they're expensive, but I tend
   to use these a lot.

4. While you're working on the lasers, have a droid scrub the
   flashback suppressors to a glossy shine. Don't ask BB-8,
   though—he might take offense.

P.O. NOTE 3478-51

Hyperdrive really takes its
toll on these babies. When
you fire up those engines, you
better hope your maintenance
guy knows what he's doing!

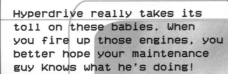

5. Can you slip a couple of half-ripe koyo fruits in with the consumables? There's nothing better on long hyperspace trips.

6. Check the coolant lines near the acceleration compensators for any leaks. I usually get them there.

7. Discharge any built-up static near the plasma combo injectors.

8. Update enemy data in the targeting computer. The First Order keeps building bigger, badder ships. I don't like surprises.

9. Don't worry about new paint—that's my job, keeping her scratch free.

10. Oil the flight controls. I like 'em loose.

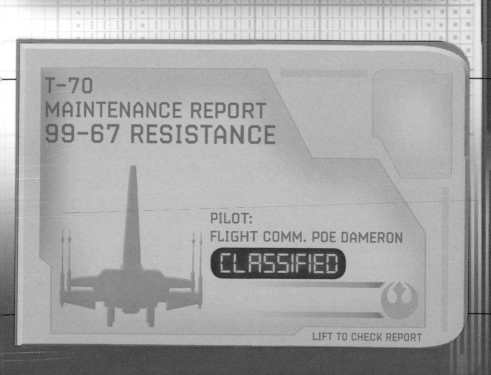

T-70
MAINTENANCE REPORT
99-67 RESISTANCE

PILOT:
FLIGHT COMM. POE DAMERON

CLASSIFIED

LIFT TO CHECK REPORT

T-70 X-WING

SIDE VIEW

Cockpit

Nose Cone

Taim & Bak KX12 Laser Cannon (4)

Technical Specifications

Model: T-70 X-wing
Manufacturer: Incom-FreiTek
Class: Starfighter
Width/Height/Depth: 12.48 m × 11.26 m × 73 m
Maximum Speed: 3,800 G (space) / 1,100 kph (atmosphere)
Hyperdrive: Class 1
Weaponry: Four laser cannons, two proton torpedo launchers
Life Support Systems: Yes
Crew: One pilot, one astromech droid
Consumables: Two-day supply

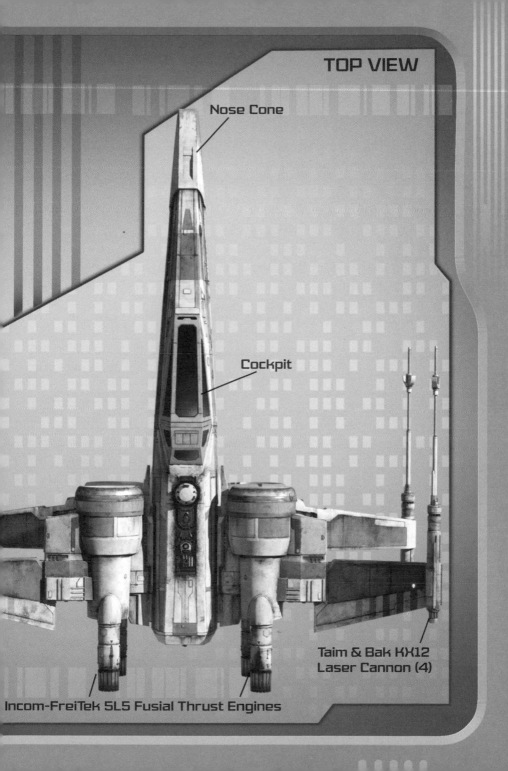

Nose Cone

Cockpit

Taim & Bak KX12
Laser Cannon (4)

Incom-FreiTek 5L5 Fusial Thrust Engines

HOLOGRAM PROJECTOR

LEIA: Commander Dameron, how is everything?

POE: Itching to land, General. Only a couple parsecs from Jakku.

LEIA: Make sure you enter the atmosphere under cover of night. Cut both active and passive scanners. Reduce power consumption to the bare minimum. No shields.

POE: You want me to go in blind?

LEIA: I want you to be as invisible as you can be. Brance is getting reports the First Order may have ships in that sector.

POE: No sweat, General. I'll slip in and out of Jakku like a cool Yavin breeze. The First Order'll never know I'm there.

LEIA: We've placed our trust in you, Poe. If we don't aquire that map and soon—

POE: Don't worry, General. You've got your best pilot on this mission.

BB-8: *BEEP-WOOORP!*

POE: And your best droid. We'll find Lor San Tekka. We'll get his map.

LEIA: May the Force be with you, Commander.

INCOMING TRANSMISSION
GENERAL ORGANA

LIFT TO
PROJECT

NAME: BB-8

MAKE: BB-series Astromech

High Frequency Antenna

Condensed Helical Transmitter

Photoreceptor

Holoprojector

Service Access Thread

Cranial Dome

P.O. NOTE 3478-52

Never know what to expect when BB-8 pops out a tool. Whether cutting blade, arc welder, or data plug, this little guy's full of surprises— and saved my backside many times.

BB-8

ESCAPE MODE

TOP VIEW

BACKGROUND: This ball-shaped astromech droid is Poe Dameron's preferred partner on missions. His orange-and-white cranial dome rests atop a similarly colored spherical body that allows him to spin and roll at top speed across a variety of terrain. While his primary function is to provide astronavigational assistance to the pilot, he has an array of tools at his disposal to conduct starfighter maintenance, data collection, and surveillance. Binary might be his main mode of communication, but he speaks it so fluently that rarely do his expressions need translation.

SHARA BEY

SHARA BEY PILOTING HER A-WING

T-70 FLIGHT RECORDER

POE: We have time to burn before arriving on Jakku, so I think I'll finish the background section of my personnel record that I've been neglecting. BB-8, can you search my datafiles and pull up holos, stills—anything that'll help spark the memory?

BB-8: *WOOOORRP?*

POE: That's a good place to start.

Mom's sense of adventure, her love of freedom—and her skill piloting anything with wings—she was my hero growing up. And to many others, too.

Her name was Shara Bey.

She grew up under the tyranny of the Galactic Empire. I don't know much about her childhood, or about her time flying for the Alliance. She wasn't the type who dwelled on the past. But get her talking about the future, and she wouldn't stop.

She said the galaxy, even during its darkest hours, was fundamentally a good place. And sometimes change is necessary to give us a jolt and remind us of what's important in life.

LOG 567-83M.64

☢ T-70 FLIGHT RECORDER

POE (continued): One of my first memories is
seeing the stars from the cockpit of my mom's
A-wing. Must've been two or three years old
at the time. I sat in her lap, straddling the flight
stick. The view of the galaxy through the
canopy has always stuck in my mind.

She even let me play a little. She told me to
be very careful with the controls . . . but you
know me, I like to test the limits—even back
then. I had to find out what the A-wing was
capable of.

After a few barrel rolls around Yavin's gas
giant, I found out Mom was right. I had to be
more careful or I'd be sick to my stomach
for days.

I'd give anything to take another flight
with her.

YAVIN 4: DAMERON HOMESTEAD

SHARA BEY'S A-WING

RZ-1 A-WING INTERCEPTOR

Sirplex Z-9
Deflector Shield
Projector

Borstel RG-9
Laser Cannons (2)

Novaldex J-77
Event Horizon
Engines

Sensor
Jamming
Array

Dymek HM-
Concussion
Missile
Launchers (2

45 DEGREE FRONT-RIGHT VIEW

45 DEGREE BACK-RIGHT VIEW

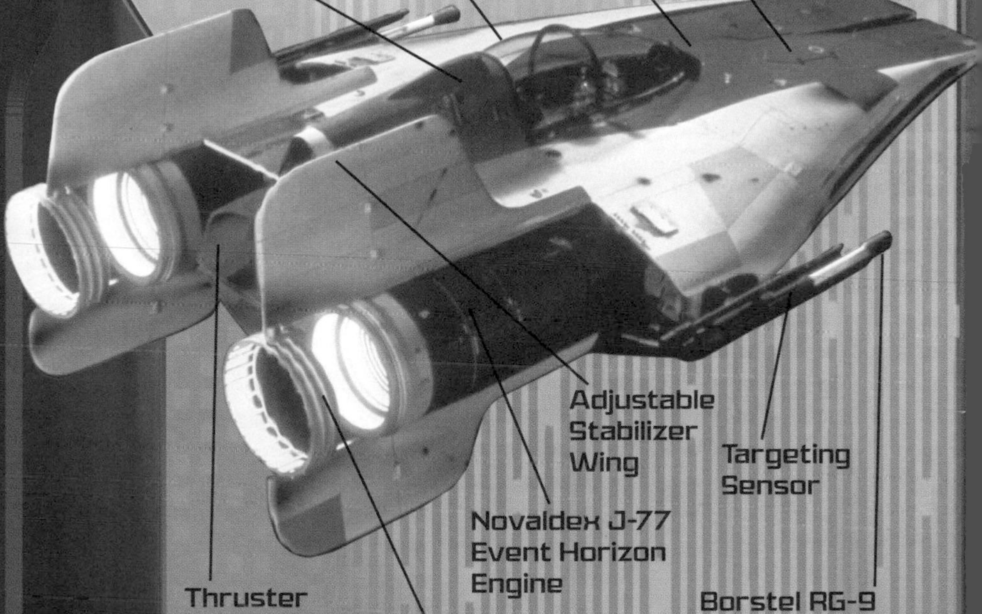

Deflector Shield Generator

Cockpit

Sensor Jamming Array

Forward Sensor Array

Access Panel

Adjustable Stabilizer Wing

Targeting Sensor

Novaldex J-77 Event Horizon Engine

Thruster Control Jets

Thrust Vector Control

Borstel RG-9 Laser Cannons (2)

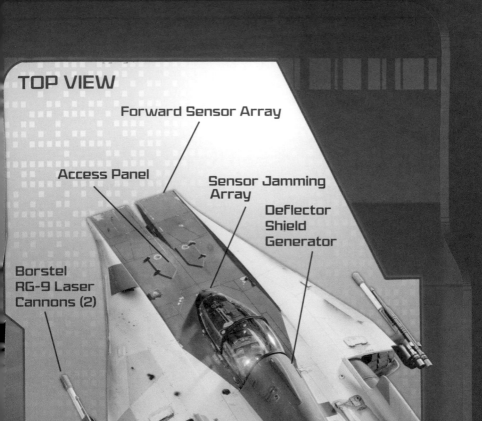

TOP VIEW

Forward Sensor Array

Access Panel

Sensor Jamming
Array

Deflector
Shield
Generator

Borstel
RG-9 Laser
Cannons (2)

Targeting
Sensor

Novaldex J-77 Event
Horizon Engines

Adjustable
Stabilizer Wing

Thruster
Control Jets

Thrust Vector
Control

Technical Specifications

Model: RZ-1 A-wing Interceptor
Manufacturer: Kuat Systems Engineering
Class: Starfighter
Length/Width/Height: 9.6 m × 6.48 m × 3.11 m
Maximum Speed: 5,100 G (space) / 1,300 kph (atmosphere)
Hyperdrive: Class 1
Weaponry: Two laser cannons, two concussion missile launchers
Shields: Yes
Life Support Systems: Yes
Crew: One pilot
Consumables: One-week supply

djustable
tabilizer Wing

Cockpit

Targeting
Sensor

Access Panel

Forward Sensor Array

P.O. NOTE 3478-53

Learned how to fly in these. Gotta
say, after all my years in an X-wing,
nothing handles like an A-wing—a
slight tap on the stick can send you
veering in the opposite direction.

Dear Kes and Poe:

I learned recently of the passing of your wife and mother.
I can only imagine your grief, and offer my sincerest
condolences.

Shara Bey was a woman like no other. The courage she
displayed to liberate Gorma won her not only the Bronze
Nova for Conspicuous Gallantry, but also the never-ending
gratitude of that world's people who had survived the
brutal Imperial occupation. Then there was her brilliant
piloting during the Battle of Endor. Did you know she
escorted my brother, Luke, to safety in that fight?

What I won't forget is the trip Shara and I had a few
months after Endor. She flew us to Naboo, where I tried to
secure Queen Sosha Soruna's support for the New Republic.
The Empire launched a surprise attack from orbit, assailing
the planet with hundreds of weather satellites that whipped
up great storms in Naboo's atmosphere. So terrible were
these storms that citizens had to flee their cities because
of flash floods and fire from lightning.

Shara, Queen Soruna, and I went up in the three
starfighters the Naboo royalty had kept hidden from the
Empire. Shara's adeptness in an N-1 fighter stunned me; it
was as if she'd flown one of those fighters since birth.
She was our leader up there, guiding us through a mission
that, if not for her, would have killed us all.

Shara had told me that if she perished during that battle above Naboo, not to write a condolence letter, as I did for the many rebels who had sacrificed their lives for our cause. But I think that was her pride talking. She refused to admit that any mission could be the end.

As long as the stars shine, Shara Bey will be remembered.

With deepest sympathy,

Senator Leia Organa
Alderaan Sector

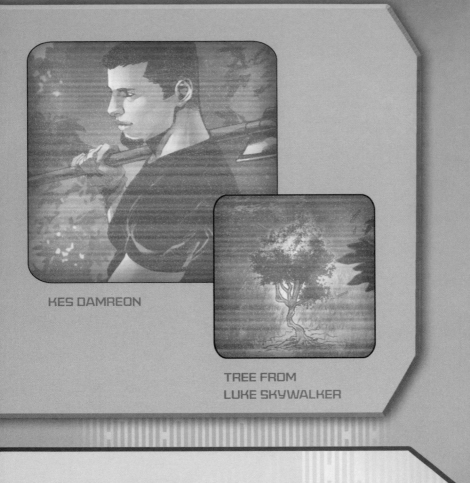

KES DAMREON

TREE FROM
LUKE SKYWALKER

POE: Mom passed when I was eight. After that, it was
just my father and me on our ranch on Yavin 4.

BB-8: *BEEP-BEEP-WOORP?*

POE: Yeah, Yavin 4's fairly peaceful . . . except when I'm
around. Used to drive my dad insane whenever I
took out the speeder for a cruise, or jumped in my
mom's RZ-1 to get away from it all.

POE (continued): Then there was the time I rigged a pair of ancient podracer engines to our koyo picker. I wanted to take a joyride in the A-wing to see a meteor shower up close, but had to do my chores first.

With those rocket engines attached, I picked the grove in a matter of minutes, compared to the hours it usually took.

Let's just say, my dad was not happy—and I never did that again.

The fiery exhaust from the podracer's engines singed the tree Luke Skywalker had given to my parents. Supposedly, it was one of the last surviving trees from the Jedi Temple on Coruscant.

BB-8: *WHHHEEEEOO!*

POE: Tell me about it. The thing was in my backyard like any other ordinary tree. As a kid, I used to swing from its branches.

Well, my dad made me spend the next year coaxing the scorched tree back to health. I learned a valuable lesson that day: Rushing through a job can cause unintended consequences.

BB-8: *WRRP-WRRP-WRRP*

POE: Yeah, patience has never been my strong suit.

BB-8: *BEEP-BREE?*

POE: What's my dad like? He's the toughest—and kindest—soldier I've ever known.

He made me into the man I am today.

Unlike my mom or me, he had no interest in being a hotshot space jockey. As he likes to say, his feet are made for boots, not flight pedals. During the war, he served in the Alliance's SpecForces as a member of their legendary Pathfinders.

BB-8: *BLEEP-BEE-BEEP?*

POE: You gotta talk to some of the older R2 units. Pathfinders were the Rebellion's first—and sometimes only—response to Imperials on the ground. They were trained in reconnaissance and infiltration, and could survive in punishing environments for weeks.

Dad's toughness was on full display whenever we'd go on long hikes through the Yavin jungles. I'd be at the point of dropping from exhaustion, but he wouldn't have broken a sweat. He always traveled light, without a tent, preferring to camp under waterfalls or in the giant fronds of jakaw trees.

Watching him track another living thing was a marvel in itself. He could spot spoors like you hear distant signals, and could pick up a trail by scent alone. I remember him dozens of meters up in the air, following the tiniest woolamander from branch to branch—just for fun.

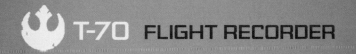

POE (continued): I can only imagine how he tracked Imperials. Scout troopers, with all their advanced gadgetry and specialized armor, stood no chance against him.

BB-8: *BEEP-BEEP*

POE: Gotcha—exiting hyperspace now. . . .

REBELS, INCLUDING MEMBERS OF THE PATHFINDERS, BEFORE THE MISSION TO ENDOR

TO: General Crix Madine
CC: Lieutenant Kes Dameron
FROM: General Han Solo
SUBJECT: Acts of Valor, etc.

TO: General Crix Madine
CC: Kes Dameron

SUBJECT: Acts of Valor, Bravery, Foolhardiness, etc.

Crix—

You know I'm not one for writing these memos. Takes too much time. But that Pathfinder kid ya got, that Kes Dameron, he makes me want to take the time.

His actions on the Ewok moon helped bring down the shield generator but he didn't stop there. He and his guys passed up partying with the furballs to mop up another Imperial base.

Yet it's what he did during our raid on the I. S. B. black site on Tayron that was nothing short of remarkable. He led the charge down the crater, straight into artillery fire. He wasn't fazed at all, and I swear one of his shots brought down a scout walker all alone. Such lunacy is something I'd do in my younger days, before I really gave two bantha ticks about my future.

(Continued)

Kes, on the other hand, already has a future—with a wife and kid of his own. Yet he ran down that crater without a second thought. We got inside that bunker 'cause of him. For once, I didn't have to be the suicidal idiot.

Look, Crix, Kes deserves some R&R. Retirement even, if that's what he wants. Don't know if you rebels give compensation packages for exemplary service, but you're welcome to use part of mine—just don't tell Chewie.

Just my two credits' worth.
—Solo

TO: General Han Solo
CC: Lieutenant Kes Dameron
FROM: General Crix Madine
SUBJECT: Re: Acts of Valor, etc.

Dameron's honorable discharge has been processed, and he has been awarded with a compensation package. Yours remains untouched.

—Crix

PLANETARY CAPSULE

JAKKU

Number of Moons: Two
Star System: Jakku
Galactic Region: Western Reaches, Inner Rim
Atmosphere: Type 1 (habitable for oxygen breathers)
Government: Local
Orbital Time Units: 352 Standard Days in a Year / 26.8 Standard Hours in a Day
Population: Unknown (less than 25,000)
Languages: Basic, Teedo, Uthuthma
Principal Terrain: Desert
Major Population Centers: Niima Outpost, Tuanul, Cratertown, Reestkii, Blowback Town
Interesting Locales: Graveyard of Starships, Sinking Fields, Kelvin Ravine, Feressee's Point, Goazon Badlands, Pilgrim's Road, Namenthe's Crater, Carbon Ridge, Niima Bazaar
Major Exports: Junk Metals, Salvaged Tech, Silicon, Bezorite, Kesium Gas, Magnite, Osmiridum
Major Imports: Water, Consumables, Luxury Goods, Technology

NIIMA BAZAAR

PILGRIM'S ROAD

SINKING FIELDS

LOG 568-IIU.40

POE: Arrived at last in the Jakku system, and approaching the planet.

As I was warned, the place looks like a globe of sandpaper.

BB-8: *WRRRP?*

POE: No, the General said no scans. I don't see any enemy craft out in the canopy. You?

BB-8: *BRRR-BRRR-WEEP*

POE: No space traffic at all. They must not get many visitors here.

NIIMA OUTPOST

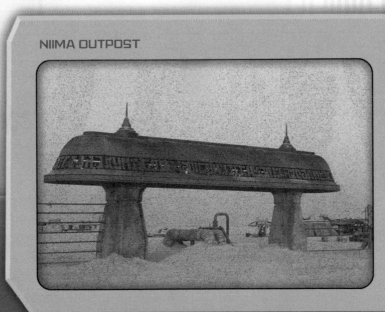

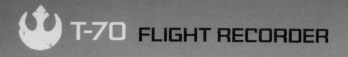

LOG 569-78P.61

POE: Took my X-wing through Jakku's nightside, then pivoted in the atmosphere and touched down near the coordinates for the village of Tuanul. This place is as bare as it looks from space.

The village isn't much more than a few bell-shaped mud huts around a wheezing vaporator. According to intelligence reports, it was founded as a spiritual community connected to something called the Church of the Force. Whatever they believe must be pretty controversial for them to live all the way in the Western Reaches. And it sure doesn't look like they're thriving. The entire settlement seems like one windstorm away from being swept into dust.

BB-8, can you get my flight jacket out of the storage compartment? It's cold out here.

BB-8: *WRRMM*

POE: Thanks. Much better. It's the simple things in life—coat, boots, blaster—that's what my dad always says.

BB-8: *MEEP?*

POE: Yes, you too, BB-8—though I'd never call you "simple." Can you do me a favor and scout the area for potential dangers? I'll keep my comlink active so you can track me.

BB-8: *BLEEP BLEEP WRRRP*

POE: Yes, I'll watch out for myself.

MISSION OBJECTIVES

Land near the village of Tuanul.
Geographic coordinates: forty-three point two hundred
ninety-one point sixty-one.

The landing place and craft should be concealed.

Jakku is a world of scavengers, and your craft could be
disassembled in minutes flat. In particular, watch out
for Teedos.

Venture into the village to locate Lor San Tekka.
Do not leave until he gives you the map.

WARNING
BEWARE OF TEEDOS

Teedos are mysterious
scavengers who roam the
wastelands of Jakku.

TEEDOS

Affiliation: None
Homeworld: Jakku
Species: Teedo
Height: 1.24 m
Occupation:
Scavengers

MAJOR BRANCE NOTE

Spies on Jakku have discovered the Tuanul village destroyed, along with Commander Dameron's X-wing. Soon after I received word of what happened, our droid network intercepted these First Order transmissions.

CAPTURED

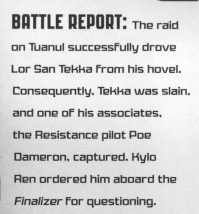

BATTLE REPORT: The raid on Tuanul successfully drove Lor San Tekka from his hovel. Consequently, Tekka was slain, and one of his associates, the Resistance pilot Poe Dameron, captured. Kylo Ren ordered him aboard the *Finalizer* for questioning.

Dameron's X-wing was seized shortly afterward, and the black box removed.

Troopers JY-834, FN-3156, FN-2198, and HX-1072 performed a deep scan of the craft. They reported finding nothing of significance.

To prevent potential allies of the pilot from escaping, I ordered the X-wing destroyed. The black box will be sent to Crypt for examination.

—Captain Phasma

Poe Dameron here . . . testing out a comm I found in the TIE . . . it semms to be recording . . . if I make it off this sandpit, do I have a story for the skyjockeys back at HQ.

Right now, I'm wandering the Jakku desert, having fled the wreckage of a TIE fighter. Before I go there, let me pick up where I left off to help keep my mind off the oppressive heat.

Many things have happened since I went searching the village for Lor San Tekka. I had no clue where to look for the man. I peeked in a few darkened windows, but saw nothing. The few beings I did pass in the streets stayed away. I didn't ask them about Tekka—you never know who can be trusted on fringe worlds like Jakku.

I made the rounds several times and was about to head back to my X-wing, when I felt a touch on my shoulder.

Lor San Tekka had found me.

LOR SAN TEKKA

TUANUL VILLAGE

LOR SAN TEKKA AND POE DAMERON

Tekka was taller than I expected—and older. He invited me inside his hut, where we made small talk. He never asked who I was, or why I was there. He knew.

Finally, he presented me with a leather pouch. "This will begin to make things right," he said.

Our conversation ended when my astromech droid, BB-8, rolled into the hut, beeping frantically. I went out to scan the skies with my quadnocs.

We had company.

BB-8 SCANNING THE SKY

STORMTROOPERS ATTACK TUANUL

LOR SAN TEKKA CAPTURED BY KYLO REN

ATMOSPHERIC ASSAULT LANDER
FRONT VIEW

Cockpit (standing)

Sienar-Jaemus
F-ZO Antipersonnel
Blaster Cannon

Xerradin IonOre
Armor Plating

Troop
Compartment

Exit Ramp

COMMAND SHUTTLE

P.D. NOTE 3478-55

I'd seen this shuttle before, heading toward the *Subjugator* while I was jetting away in an AAL with Ackbar. When it landed on Jakku, I knew I was in for a world of trouble.

Technical Specifications

Model: Shuttle

HEIGHT: 37.2 meters

ARMAMENT: Two twin laser cannons

ATMOSPHERIC ASSAULT LANDER

Technical Specifications

Model: Atmospheric Assault Lander
Manufacturer: Sienar-Jaemus Army Systems
Class: Transport
Width/Height/Depth: 18.05 m × 6.3 m × 6.05 m
Maximum Speed: 1,900 G (space) / 900 kph (atmosphere)
Hyperdrive: none
Weaponry: One blaster cannon (dorsal)
Shields: Yes
Life Support Systems: Yes
Crew: One pilot, one gunner, two stormtrooper squads (twenty troopers)
Consumables: Three-day supply for two trooper squads

P.O. NOTE 3478-54

I've flown AAL transports in the past. Not much more than heavily armored crates. Main cockpit's a tiny closet elevated like a fin—an easy target—though the craft can also be operated from inside the troop compartment, which is what I did. Thankfully, mine didn't carry a full complement of twenty bucketheads.

Cockpit (standing)

SJAS-210 Sublight Engines

Xerradin IonOre Armor Plating

Troop Compartment

Never made it off Jakku in my X-wing—stormtroopers shot up the engine. I shot back, but it was only a matter of time before I was captured or killed like the villagers. There were just too many stormtroopers.

I didn't care about my own life. What mattered were the map, General Organa, and the Resistance.

I took the old data storage device from the pouch and fed it into BB-8's memory slot. Then I told him to get as far away as he could.

Of course, he wouldn't listen. His loyalty subprogram wouldn't allow him to leave me alone with the First Order. He went only when I promised to come back for him.

Some might say he's just a droid, but I felt a pang of regret watching BB-8 roll away. I doubted I could keep that promise.

That doubt has grown the longer I bake on Jakku. If only I could find some water. . . .

T-70 DAMAGE REPORT
CATASTROPHIC ENGINE DAMAGE

BB-8 RECEIVING THE STORAGE DEVICE

DECEASED

Name: Lor San Tekka
Species: Human
Gender: Male
Homeworld: Unknown

Background: Much of Tekka's past remains a mystery. What is known is that he was born during the waning years of the Republic, and as a young man, he became interested in the Jedi Knights. Though he shared none of their legendary powers, he joined fellow enthusiasts in an organization called the Church of the Force, where Jedi history was studied and celebrated.

When the Empire took over, Tekka became an explorer, risking capital punishment by researching sites of significance to the Jedi. He uncovered many of their artifacts and saved them from destruction by Imperial archaeologists. Yet his discoveries forced him to run from the authorities and to avoid capture by never spending too much time in one place.

Both Resistance and First Order intelligence agents have been hot on the trail of Tekka for years. But whenever and wherever he surfaced, such as with the Ottegans on Arthon, he would soon disappear before he could be found. Recently, Resistance pilot Poe Dameron began searching for Tekka under the directive of General Organa. He learned that Tekka had lived briefly with a community on Ovanis who called themselves the Crèche. They protected an egg they thought would hatch a "savior" that would bring an end to all ills in the galaxy. Tekka, however, was long gone.

Further investigation led Dameron to the prison world of Megalox Beta and the incarcerated Hutt crime boss Grakkus. Dameron foiled a similar probe by Agent Terex of the First Order, and forced Grakkus to reveal what he knew concerning Tekka's possible whereabouts. Only after more hard work on the part of Dameron and the Resistance intelligence services was Tekka traced to Jakku. There the man dwelled with a collective of like-minded spirituals in the village of Tuanul. Before his death, Tekka gave his greatest artifact to Dameron: a map that might lead to the lost Jedi Master Luke Skywalker.

"Without the Jedi," he told Dameron, "there can be no balance in the Force."

P.O. NOTE 3478-56

Tekka was murdered by that masked madman, Kylo Ren. I witnessed it when I returned to the village. With one vicious swing of Ren's lightsaber, Lor San Tekka fell like so many of his Jedi heroes.

I fired immediately at Ren. The shot should've killed him, except it never reached him—he gestured and the blaster bolt froze midair.

Then I was seized by stormtroopers.

P.O. NOTE 3478-57

Troopers shuttled me to the Star Destroyer that orbited Jakku. I overheard them calling it *Finalizer*. After the torture I endured in the detention cell, I think it's a fitting name.

P.D. NOTE 3478-5B

C-3PO gave this to me, thinking I
might find it of interest. He received
it from another protocol droid in his
spy network. I didn't ask questions,
since I didn't want to know.

INTERROGATOR: IT-000—XZ 1594

SUBJECT: YL032/767—Interrogation of Prisoner 8910542

REPORT TRANSLATED AND LOGGED BY: RA-7-D4

Prisoner 8910542, also known as Poe Dameron, a starfighter
squadron commander for the Resistance, was taken from Jakku
to holding cell 64949 on the Star Destroyer *Finalizer*.

IT-000 unit XZ 1594 was instructed to use all available techniques
to determine the location of a map the prisoner had to a highly
sought-after enemy of the First Order named Luke Skywalker.

The prisoner refused to answer the question about the map's
location. The IT unit repeated the question 813 times. The prisoner
spit at the droid in response.

The IT unit proceeded to apply methods 2265, 6304, 3333, and
K8-A4 to the prisoner. The prisoner reacted violently to procedure
K8-A4, and nearly swallowed his tongue. The IT unit increased the
neuroshock amplitude and repeated the question: Where is the
map to Luke Skywalker?

Kylo Ren strode into the cell and shoved the droid aside.

Ren used no probing device in his interrogation. He extended his hand before the prisoner's face and asked the question.

Where is the map to Luke Skywalker?

The prisoner twisted in his bonds. He refused to answer the question and said the Resistance will not be intimidated.

Then he screamed.

The prisoner's scream was so voluminous that it shattered the IT-000's sensory capsules. The unit has recorded nothing since the interrogation.

I've been walking the desert now for hours. There's no sign of civilization. No sign of water. I'm badly sunburned and feel stupid for leaving my jacket in the TIE fighter. Could've used it for shade.

As horrible as Jakku is, it's nothing compared to what Kylo Ren did. His fingers never even touched my skin, but somehow burrowed into my brain, my blasted *mind*.

That ghoul took my secrets.

He ripped from my mind what I couldn't hold back—that I had hidden the map inside BB-8.

I was left shaking in the chair. I thought I was dead. I thought I had doomed the Resistance, the galaxy.

But I should've remembered what my mother said about the galaxy being fundamentally a good place, even in the darkest times.

Because that's when a stormtrooper—a First Order stormtrooper—opened the cell door and rescued me.

Next thing I know, I'm flying a Special Forces TIE fighter back to Jakku.

FN-2187 RESCUING POE

POE AND FN-2187
STEALING A SPECIAL
FORCES TIE FIGHTER

SF TIE FIGHTER

Technical Specifications

Model: TIE/sf space superiority fighter
Manufacturer: Sienar-Jaemus Fleet Systems
Class: Starfighter
Width/Height/Depth: 6.69 m ×
6.34 m × 8.17 m
Maximum Speed: 4,100 G (space) / 1,200 kph
(atmosphere)
Hyperdrive: Class 3
Weaponry: One laser turret,
two laser cannons, concussion
and mag-pulse warhead launcher
Shields: Yes
Life Support Systems: Yes
Crew: One pilot, one gunner
Consumables: One-week supply

FRONT-SIDE VIEW

Pilot's Forward Viewport

Cockpit

Reinforced Alloy Wing Pylon

Lb-14 Dual Laser Turret 360-degree Field of Fire

L-s9.6 Laser Cannons, Front Facing (2)

Solar Panel (girondium-colium collectors)

P.O. NOTE 3478-59

Always wanted to fly one of these. Had done so in simulations, but never the real thing. I'm sure First Order pilots dream the same about X-wings. Survive as many dogfights as I have and you'll develop a grudging respect for your opposition—and curiosity. Is it the craft that's good, or the pilot?

FRONT VIEW

Communications Antenna

l-a4b Solar Ionization Reactor

Hatch (top)

Ps-6 Twin Ion Engines

There's something worse than the blazing heat of Jakku's sun—the freezing cold of its night.

Would do anything to have my jacket.

I'm resting under a boulder, avoiding most of the chilly breeze, but shivering all the same. Man, only a single rotation has passed since the attack on Tuanul. . . .

Some water would be good, too. . . .

Where did I leave off? The TIE . . . I was piloting the TIE out of the destroyer's hangar . . . the trooper was with me . . . FN-2187 . . . or as I dubbed him, Finn.

I hate how the First Order turns soldiers into numbers, as if they were no different from a T-70 or a Z-95. Expendable.

I wanted to go back to Jakku for BB-8. Finn didn't. The *Finalizer* settled our debate. We got hit—bad. I blacked out.

When I came to, Finn had ejected. And the TIE was on a crash-course for Jakku.

Instincts took over. I yanked back on the flight yoke. The TIE bucked, leveled, skimmed the tops of sand dunes. Slowed it down, just enough. When it crashed, it did so at an angle, crumpling a wing—yet not the whole cockpit. The sands cushioned the crash.

I crawled out and never looked back.

THE STOLEN SPECIAL FORCES TIE FIGHTER AFTER CRASHING ON JAKKU

FN-2187

STORMTROOPER FN-2187

COMBAT SIMULATION
SCORE: 87

MENTAL PREPAREDNESS: 5

DIVISION: SANITATION

COMMANDER:CAPTAIN PHASMA

FN-2187
ALSO GOES BY "FINN"

FN-2187 AND POE DAMERON ESCAPED FROM
THE *FINALIZER* IN A SPECIAL FORCES
TIE FIGHTER AND HEADED FOR JAKKU

BACKGROUND: Considered a model stormtrooper, FN-2187 graduated near the top of his class and was well regarded by everyone in the corps, from his commandant to his peers. In recent mission simulations and arena melees, he proved his mettle time and again as one of the best combat soldiers. He always respected his superiors and followed orders to the letter—until he went to Jakku. He couldn't fire at defenseless civilians. What his comrades did sickened him.

When he returned to the *Finalizer*, he made a choice. He turned his back on the First Order and freed Commander Dameron from detention.

NAME: FN-2187

SPECIES: Human

GENDER: Male

FN-2187 WAS UNABLE TO
COMPLETE HIS MISSION IN TUANAL

P.O. NOTE 3478-60

When I asked Finn why he
was helping me, a sworn
enemy, his answer was simple:
It was the right thing to do.
Imagine that ...

Still no water. And I hurt. All over. From the walking. The heat of another day. The torture.

I feel pain even in my teeth.

Just need to keep talking. Remind myself I'm still alive.

How much longer that'll be, no idea.

Sorry, BB-8.

If you have come across my remains and are listening to this, bring my log back to New Republic or Resistance authorities. The galaxy might depend on it.

I can barely see now. My eyes sting. The salt. The sun. One of its rays speeds toward me. Perhaps this is the end . . .

Or is it . . . a speeder?

OVER HERE!

SPECIES: Blarina

Although the species appears to be weak and helpless, they are actually rugged and resourceful beings. Blarina have tough skin and can survive heat, cold, and decompression, and are resistant to poison and desease.

NAME: Naka Iit
SPECIES: Blarina
GENDER: Male
HOMEWORLD: Rina Major

P.O. NOTE 347B-61

Dredged up info on the two Blarina who helped get me off Jakku. Naka Iit drove me in his speeder to Blowback Town, where I hitched a ride to Yavin 4 with his buddy, Ohn Gos. Amazing how the kindness of strangers keeps me alive. I'll remember these two, as grumpy as they were—beings like this are worth fighting for.

BACKGROUND: A Blarina of this name used to race pods, and on a number of occasions placed in the top five in Lolo Cochee's Speedster Challenge on Malastare. An injury sustained from a crash in one race seems to have resulted in Iit giving up podracing for good, though other reports indicate he was caught trying to fix a race with the bookie Ohn Gos. The two fled the authorities on Malastare, where conviction of manipulating a podrace carries the death penalty, and arrived on faraway Jakku. Iit found he enjoyed the freedom of a scavenger's life, flitting about the desert and searching the scrap heaps for materials he could sell.

NAME: Ohn Gos

SPECIES: Blarina

GENDER: Male

HOMEWORLD:
Rina Major

As payment for the ride, Gos picked koyo melons from the orchard at my family ranch—said he'd make a fortune back on Jakku. The scavengers there will devour anything, especially these babies.

BACKGROUND: Before turning to the import-export business on Jakku, Ohn Gos catered to rich Hutts and profligate aristocrats as a podracing bets-maker. Wanting more than just a nice living, he masterminded an elaborate scheme to fix the outcome of the 432nd edition of Lolo Cochee's Speedster Challenge on Malastare. Everything was happening according to plan, with his partner-in-crime, Naka Iit, playing tricks on some fellow racers to fix the order of winners. Then, the harmonic dampener on Iit's podracer spun out of harmony and triggered a massive pileup that reversed the order.

Needless to say, Gos's plans were discovered on the computer of Iit's wrecked podracer. Gos and Iit fled prosecution in a derelict freighter Gos bought off the black market. Neither were skilled astrogators, so Gos used whatever coordinates were stored in the navicomputer—and exited hyperspace at the ship's last location, Jakku.

On this remote world, Gos discovered a knack for appraising salvage. He now runs a lucrative trading business using the freighter, which he renamed *Beloved Bophine*.

POE: So much has happened since my last log.

I lifted off Yavin 4 in *Black One*, which I had left at the ranch before departing for Jakku in an unmarked X-wing. The other astromech assigned to my mission, RO-H2, did a good job keeping *Black One* in tip-top shape despite the humid Yavin climate.

I didn't have time to dictate another log, because Admiral Statura had me shooting off to join a strike force at Takodana.

BB-8 had been found there . . . with Finn and Han Solo!

We fought off the First Order from Maz Kanata's castle—but were caught off-guard by a more heinous act.

Without provocation or warning, the First Order obliterated the capital of the New Republic—the Hosnian star system—with their superweapon.

Starkiller Base.

THE STARKILLER BASE FIRING
ON HOSNIAN STAR SYSTEM

LIFT TO PROJECT

INCOMING TRANSMISSION
STARKILLER BATTLE PLAN

PILOTING *BLACK ONE*

POE (continued): Now I'm doing light-speed loops around Starkiller Base, awaiting the order for my squadrons to strike . . . this may be my last entry for a while. . . .

BB-8: *BEEP!*

POE: No—not ever. We'll make it through this, despite what C-3PO says about the odds.

Just overjoyed you're in the socket again . . . wouldn't fly this mission with any other droid.

BB-8: *MEEP-MEEP-WRRR*

POE: Before we arrive, can you transmit a copy of my updated log to Yavin 4? At least then my dad will have an honest record of what happened to me, if all goes south. . . .

BB-8: *BROOO-WRRRP*

POE: Loud and clear, BB-8. Patch the Admiral through.

REAR ADMIRAL GUICH: Black Leader, Starkiller's shield is down. Go to sub-lights. Attack—repeat—attack on your call.

POE: Roger, Base.

Knew Finn would bring down that shield!

BB-8: *MEEP-MEEP-WRROO*

POE: Red Squad, Blue Squad, follow my lead . . .

BLUE SQUADRON PROFILES

NAME: Snap Wexly ("Blue One")

SPECIES: Human

GENDER: Male

HOMEWORLD: Akiva

ASTROMECH DROID: R6-D8

NAME: Yolo Ziff ("Blue Two")

SPECIES: Human

GENDER: Male

ASTROMECH DROID: M9-G8

WEXLEY REVIEWING THE ATTACK ON STARKILLER BASE

NAME: Jess "Testor" Pava ("Blue Three")

SPECIES: Human

GENDER: Female

HOMEWORLD: Dandoran

ASTROMECH DROID: RO-4LO <<ROLO>>

RED SQUADRON PROFILES

NAME: Nien Nunb ("Red Three")

SPECIES: Sullustan

GENDER: Male

HOMEWORLD: Sullust

ASTROMECH DROID: RP-GO

NAME: Ello Asty ("Red Six")

SPECIES: Abednedo

GENDER: Male

HOMEWORLD: Abedne—

ASTROMECH DROID: Unknown

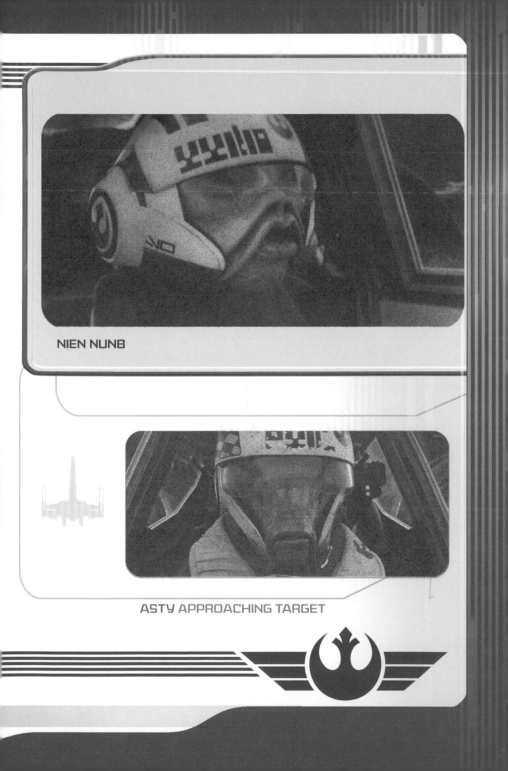

NIEN NUNB

ASTY APPROACHING TARGET

POE: Just want to set the record straight.

People always want a poster boy after any incredible feat is accomplished. But I don't want to be that face. Because what happened at Starkiller Base wasn't the work of one pilot, or one daring deed, or one shot in a million—what we did at Starkiller, we did as a team.

Here's how it went down.

We were losing . . . real bad. Our bombing runs failed to blast open the containment complex. Even after all the tonnage we dropped, there was barely a dent. It was impenetrable.

Yet, if we didn't destroy the oscillator it housed, the Starkiller weapon would annihilate the D'Qar system into its original elements.

LOG 575-35F.79

DAMERON APPROACHING THE TARGET

FINN'S TEAM

POE (continued): The light in the sky was nearly gone. The Starkiller weapon had almost completely drained the sun. And the weapon would be at full charge in minutes.

We were pummeled by laserfire. Targeted by seeker drones. Swarmed by wave after wave of TIEs. No amount of jinking and juking can save ace pilots when they're overwhelmed starboard-to-port, bow-to-stern.

There was little my squadrons could do.

Ello and Furillo died in those dark skies, lost in the fire of combat. You see a flash, hear a boom— sometimes an astromech's squeal over the comm— then, they're gone. No goodbyes.

Their sacrifices were not in vain . . . they bought us precious time. Because just when it looked like everything was doomed, the roof of the containment complex blew—from the inside.

Finn's team had infiltrated the center on the ground and given us an opportunity.

We wouldn't have another go at this. Time was running out before the Starkiller fired.

I ordered my wingmates to pull up and cover me. Then, I closed my S-foils and dove my X-wing through the breach.

A single TIE pursued.

He didn't make it.

WEXLEY: Black Leader, we've lost visual contact— repeat we've lost visual contact—

DAMERON: I'm fine, Snap. Got through the breach— now inside the oscillator shaft . . .

static

DAMERON: Blue One, Blue Three, do you read me? Do you read me?

more static

JESS: —in and out, Black Leader—

DAMERON: Duracrete layers must be blocking transmission. Beebee-Ate, you recording this?

BB-8: *BEEP!*

DAMERON: Good—we need to capture as much data about this place as we can for the Resistance. Now, where are the containment field regulators?

BB-8: *WRRREEE-BEEP-BLEEP!*

P.D. NOTE 3478-63

I cut-and-pasted this comm transcript into my log from the official record, so when I read this years later, I can be sure of the truth and not the myth.

DAMERON: I see one—

PEW—PEW—BOOM!

DAMERON: Gone!

WEXLEY: . . . more seeker drones launched . . .

JESS: Commander . . . skies nearly pitch black—

DAMERON: Just keep your fingers on those
        triggers, I'm gonna do the same.

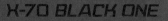

X-70 BLACK ONE

BLACK ONE FLIGHT RECORDER

DAMERON: Targets acquired—torpedoes launched—

PEW—PEW—PEW—PEW

DAMERON: Swinging around to hit the last
regulator . . . done!

*BOOM-BOOM-BOOM-BOOM-BOOOOM-
BOOM—CRAAAACK!!!*

DAMERON: Red and Blue Squadrons, they're down! Repeat, the containment shields are down!

BB-8: *BREE-WRRRRPP*

DAMERON: And Beebee-Ate's confirmed the chain reaction has started!

WEXLEY: We see it here, too—get outta there, Poe, before the oscillator blows!

DAMERON: Ditto on that, Snap. Whole place is collapsing—cover me on ascent—

BB-8: *WHEEEE-OOOO!*

DAMERON: Quite a light show in these skies now . . .

BB-8: *WRRP-WRRP-WRRP*

JESS: You did it, Black Leader, you did it!

DAMERON: No, *we* did it! Let's find the *Falcon* and take this party home, friends.

BB-8: *BEEP-WRRRRR-BEEP!*

DAMERON: Told you we'd beat those odds, little buddy. No matter what the First Order hurls at us, they're not going to win. We've got the galaxy on our side.

BLACK ONE FLIGHT RECORDER

LOG 576-64B.48T

POE: There's a lifetime's worth of adventures collected here, and I'm ready to take a break from logging.

Not for long, I suspect.

If there's one thing I've learned through all this, it's that trouble never rests.

But neither does Poe Dameron.

Signing off, for now.

RESISTANCE

FLIGHT COMMANDER

T-70 X-WING
BLACK ONE

STATUS: ACTIVE
LEVEL 9

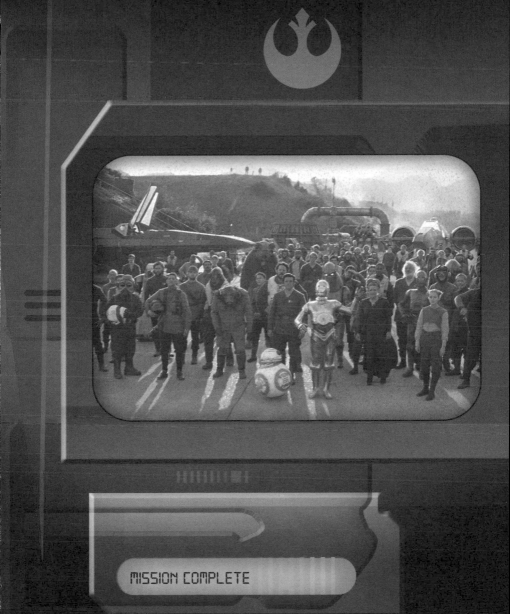

MISSION COMPLETE

Writer: Michael Kogge

Editor: Amy Nathanson Heaslip

Art Director and Designer: Andrew Barthelmes

Page Layout: Rebecca Stone

Copy Editor: Mary Bronzini-Klein

Managing Editor: Christine Guido

Creative Director: Julia Sabbagh

Associate Publisher: Rosanne McManus

Lucasfilm Editors: Brett Rector, Frank Parisi

Creative Director, Lucasfilm: Michael Siglain

Lucasfilm Story Group: Leland Chee, Pablo Hidalgo, Matt Martin

Published by Studio Fun International, Inc.

44 South Broadway, White Plains, NY 10601 U.S.A. and

Studio Fun International Limited, Bath, UK

All rights reserved. Studio Fun Books is a trademark

of Studio Fun International, Inc., a subsidiary of

Trusted Media Brands, Inc.

Printed in China.

Conforms to ASTM F963 and EN 71

10 9 8 7 6 5 4 3 2 1

SL2/08/16

RESISTANCE ISSUED 984D843X